THE GENTLEMAN BAT

by Abraham Schroeder

illustrated by Piotr Parda

Ripple Grove Press

First Edition 2014
Library of Congress Control Number 2014933037
ISBN 978-0-9913866-0-4

2 4 6 8 10 9 7 5 3 1

Printed in the USA

This book was typeset in Caslon.
The illustrations were done in watercolor, bamboo pen, and ink.
Characters by Abraham Schroeder and Piotr Parda
Cover design by Piotr Parda and Abraham Schroeder
Cover and title page typefaces by Piotr Parda

Ripple Grove Press
Visit us at www.RippleGrovePress.com

For Kait and Nathaniel
-A. S.

For Lisa
-P. P.

And for all the bats around the world

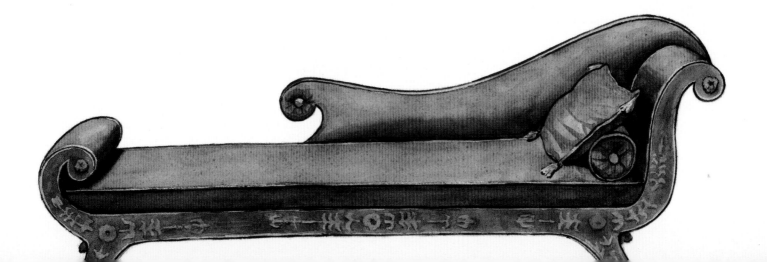

The gentleman bat, with his gentleman's cane,
Went out for a walk one night in the rain.

With his gentleman's shoes and his gentleman's spats,
He made quite a sight to the top of his hat.

The gentleman bat kept his clothes trim and neat;
His shiny shoes tapped on the cobblestone street.

The full moon was shining, the temperature fair;
A wispy grey fog infused the crisp air.

The cool autumn drizzle did not spoil his stroll;
A sprinkling of rain can be good for the soul.

Gaslights burned brightly to fend off the dark;
Soft music drifted across the town park.

The street was not crowded, nor was it bare.
The gentleman made his way to the town square.

With a nod of his head and a wink of his eye,
The gentleman bat would greet passersby.

As he walked down the street, he saw up round the bend
A young lady bat whom he knew as a friend.

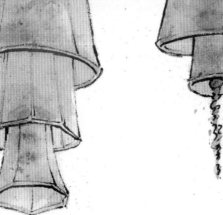

The lady bat walked in her blue satin gown,
Covered with ribbons and frills spilling down.

Her patent-shined boots were laced up to the knee;
Fine pearl-rimmed spectacles helped her to see.

He smiled at her fondly and bowed low in greeting.
"Good evening," he said, and "Fancy us meeting!"

The two of them walked down the street side by side,
But not very close – her hoopskirt was wide.

The square by the fountain had lively performers,
Artists, and vendors on all the street corners.

The shops in the market had goods on display.
The band in the bandstand started to play.

The gentleman bat asked the lady to dance:
A gentleman's way to kindle romance.

The gentleman bat took the lady bat's hand;
They twirled for a while to the sound of the band.

He spun her around and dipped her down low;
She giggled and laughed and kicked up her toe.

Before long the final song faded out lightly.
He bowed and she curtsied; he thanked her politely.

The two bats continued their nice evening walk,
To stroll hand in hand, to smile and to talk.

Without any warning came cause for concern:
The sky took a sinister, foreboding turn.

The moon was obscured by an ominous cloud,
And blowing through trees, the wind's howling grew loud.

The gentle night rain that had fallen before,
With a loud clap of thunder, became a downpour!

The lady bat's bonnet, covered in feathers,
Started to droop because of the weather!

The gentleman bat, without blinking an eye,
Grabbed his cane quickly and held it up high!

The cane was carved teak, with exotic designs;
A lever was hidden among the small lines.

The lever attached to a hook and a spring
To cause an umbrella to pop from the thing!

The clever umbrella sprung out from the cane,
Protecting the bats from the sudden rain.

The evening was rescued, no reason to cry;
The lady bat's hat was now covered and dry.

The oilcloth deflected the brunt of the storm;
They cuddled together, now cozy and warm.

The storm soon calmed down to a pleasanter shower.
The two bats meandered around the clock tower.

They strolled a bit more, but the hour was late;
The gentleman escorted her to her gate.

They lingered a moment under a streetlight.
She offered her cheek and he kissed her good night.

Their hearts fluttered wistfully as he departed,
And made his way back to his house where he started.

The gentleman bat, with his gentleman's cane,
Had finished his walk that night in the rain.

He hung his hat neatly on the hook by the door,
Set his wet shoes and spats on the mat on the floor.

The clever umbrella he opened to dry,
As a sliver of sun was tickling the sky.

He closed the drapes tightly to keep out the dawn,
And stretched his wings wide with a gentleman's yawn.

The gentleman bat, at the end of the night,
Put on his nightcap and turned out the light.